WiLLA and WOOF

Books by Jacqueline Harvey

Willa and Woof series
Mimi is Missing

Kensy and Max series

Alice-Miranda series

Clementine Rose series

That Cat

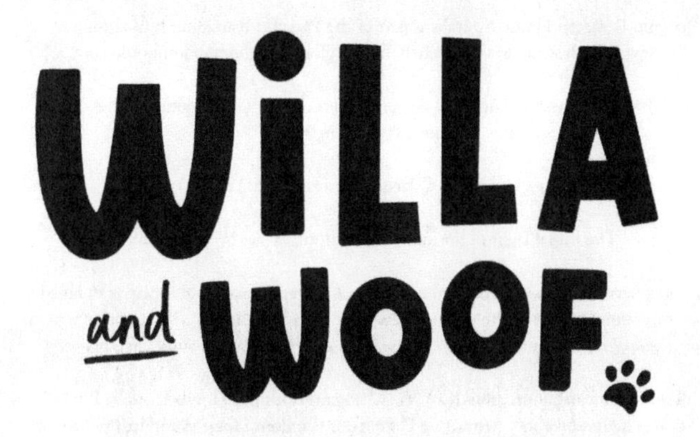

Mimi is Missing

JACQUELINE HARVEY

Illustrations by A. Yi

PUFFIN BOOKS

PUFFIN BOOKS

UK | USA | Canada | Ireland | Australia
India | New Zealand | South Africa | China

Penguin Random House Australia is part of the Penguin Random House group of companies whose addresses can be found at global.penguinrandomhouse.com.

First published by Puffin Books, an imprint of Penguin Random House Australia Pty Ltd, in 2022

Printed and bound in Australia by Griffin Press, part of Ovato, an accredited ISO AS/NZS 14001 Environmental Management Systems printer

A catalogue record for this book is available from the National Library of Australia

ISBN 978 1 76 104331 4 (Paperback)

Penguin Random House Australia uses papers that are natural and recyclable products, made from wood grown in sustainable forests. The logging and manufacture processes are expected to conform to the environmental regulations of the country of origin.

penguin.com.au

We at Penguin Random House Australia acknowledge that Aboriginal and Torres Strait Islander peoples are the Traditional Custodians and the first storytellers of the lands on which we live and work. We honour Aboriginal and Torres Strait Islander peoples' continuous connection to Country, waters, skies and communities. We celebrate Aboriginal and Torres Strait Islander stories, traditions and living cultures; and we pay our respects to Elders past and present.

For Phoebe Rose, who loves dogs
(and everyone and everything else!)

CHAPTER ONE

Woof

My name is Willa and I want to introduce you to Woof. He's my dog. His real name is Wilfred Connal Tate, but when I was little 'Wilfred' never came out right. Mum and Dad thought it was cute that I called him Woof, so it stuck.

I have three best friends. Woof is my best four-legged friend. My best same-age friend is Tae Jin, but everyone just calls him Tae. My best old-age friend is Frank.

His last name is Pickles, which is funny because he *loves* eating pickles on his sandwiches. I'm not a fan.

Frank is *very* old and *very* grumpy. He has crinkly skin and bags under his eyes. Sometimes when Woof and I visit him he tells us to go home. But I don't, because my grandma says that I'm good company and my dad says that my grandma knows everything. It never takes long for Frank to be less grumpy and maybe even smile – especially if I tell him a joke.

He makes me cracker biscuits with peanut butter, and lime cordial with ice cubes. Some days there's cakes that Frank says he's cooked, but I know he hasn't. His neighbour, Mrs Best, brings them over in her Tupperware containers. Frank has a special bag of treats for Woof too.

When I visit, which is pretty much every day, Frank tells me stories. I don't always know if they're true, but I hope they are. I tell Frank everything that goes on at school and at home. I love to make him laugh, but that's like winning the lottery. It doesn't happen very often and, as my mum says, the odds are against you – whatever that means.

Before Frank came to live at Sunset Views – that's the name of the retirement village, which is next door to our house at the end of Cricklewood Crescent – he had more than fifty pets. That's at least forty-nine more than me. But they were all the same. Pigeons.

Dad says Frank was a 'pigeon fancier', which means he liked them a lot (not just that they're fancy birds). He has pigeon mugs and pigeon plates, pigeon wall

hangings and pigeon paintings, and even a pigeon clock.

Frank's pigeons used to go in races, and not just against each other. There were pigeons from everywhere. A truck would drive them far away – at least one hundred kilometres and sometimes even one thousand – and then they would fly home. The first one back was the winner. He says that they're the racehorses of the sky.

The pigeons didn't win gold medals like my brother, Sam, did when his cricket team won their grand final. Instead, they won all the pigeon stuff Frank has in his house.

I don't think pigeons would care that much about mugs and clocks. I'm sure they'd rather win birdseed, and swings and mirrors for the aviary.

Fifty pigeons cooing and pooing in the same cage would be *very* loud and *very* messy. So it's lucky Frank only has one pigeon now. Her name is Mimi. She's grey with shiny purple and green feathers on her neck. But there's a big problem.

Mimi is missing.

CHAPTER TWO

A Secret

Mimi is missing because of me.

Two days ago I was helping Frank clean out her aviary, which is really just a big cage in his back garden next to a little shed. When we were done, I closed the door but I couldn't get the latch to hook properly. I meant to tell Frank, but then I got distracted showing him how to do cartwheels and round offs (I even did one over Woof and he's almost the tallest dog in the world) and then I forgot.

I haven't told anyone and now it feels as if I've swallowed a rock. A big, sharp-edged one that's cutting my insides to pieces.

If anything happens to Mimi I don't know what I'll do. She's really precious to Frank, like Woof is to me.

Woof went missing once, but then he howled so loudly it didn't take long to find him. He was accidentally locked in the Woods' garage next door. They live on the other side of our house to Frank. Dad said it might *not* have been an accident because their teenage son, Michael, is always trying to steal Woof. That's because he's an albino

Irish wolfhound, which is pretty rare. He's also the best dog in the world.

I found out that Mimi was gone yesterday when I went to visit Frank after school. I knocked on the back door, same as I always do, and a lady answered.

She said Frank was doing a test, which is weird because he finished school about a hundred years ago.

I said I could wait, but the lady shook her head and tapped on her clipboard, so I walked to the aviary to say hello to Mimi. That's when I saw she was missing and remembered about the latch.

Now I'm walking up and down the street looking for her. Again.

'Mimi!' I shout. 'Coo, coo.'

A magpie warbles and a cockatoo screeches, but there are no pigeons.

A silver car drives past and parks at the two-storey house across the road from us. It's Tae and his mum, Soo-Min. Tae's wearing a fireman's hat. I give him a wave.

'What are you doing, Willa?' Tae calls as he hops out of the car.

'Looking for Mimi,' I call back. I told

him she was missing last night (our families had a barbecue). 'Do you want to help?'

'Sure,' he yells. 'Would you like me to bring a ladder?'

I frown and check the street before I run across to Tae's driveway. There's never many cars because it's a cul-de-sac.

'No. We can come back for it later, *if* we find her.'

'But a fireman always has a ladder,' Tae says. 'And this week I'm a fireman.'

The name Tae means 'person of greatness' in Korean.

Ever since I can remember, Tae's been trying to decide what sort of person of greatness he's going to be. Last week he was a cowboy and next week he'll be something else.

I think he puts too much pressure on himself. After all, he just turned eight last month. At his party I gave him a policeman's uniform, which he loved. When I turned eight in March, Tae gave me a koala diary and pen. I write all my secrets and plans inside.

Tae is the youngest kid in our year. Soo-Min says maybe she should have kept him back, but he would have been so sad if I went to school without him. And it doesn't matter, because he's smarter than almost everyone in our class.

Tae and I walk along the footpath, looking up at the trees and the rooftops.

'Pigeons like to walk on the ground as well,' Tae says.

I gasp. What if Mimi has been run over by a car or eaten by Mrs Best's cat, Ginger Biscuit? He's a serial killer.

Rats, mice, birds – that cat is a menace to the neighbourhood. Now I feel sick.

'Have you seen Frank today?' Tae asks.

I shake my head. I don't want to see him until Mimi is back where she belongs. Frank used to have another pigeon called Norman, but he disappeared when I was four. I don't remember much about him though and Frank won't talk about what happened.

'Probably for the best,' Tae says.

I look at him. What does *he* know?

'Mum says that Frank was snappier than a crocodile last night.'

The rock in my stomach grows twice as big. Soo-Min is a nurse at the retirement village. One of her jobs is to visit the residents to make sure that they're taking their medicines and eating properly.

'Come on.' I scan the blue sky again. 'I've got a plan.'

CHAPTER THREE

The Plan

I grab Tae's hand and we run down the side of my house, to the gate in the fence that goes straight to Frank's villa.

Woof is lying down on the grass but he quickly jumps up and runs to meet us. I ruffle his head and straighten his coat. He gets sunburnt really easily – even in winter – so he wears a coat most of the time. He has lots in different colours (Woof's a very fashionable dog).

We have to put sunscreen on his nose too.

Tae kneels down to give Woof a cuddle.

'What are we doing?' Tae asks.

'I need to borrow something from Frank,' I tell him.

'I'll just wait here with Woof,' Tae says.

I was expecting that. Tae hardly ever comes to visit Frank with me.

'But I need you to keep a lookout,' I say.

Tae shakes his head. 'I can watch from here.'

Seriously, that is not going to happen.

'No you can't,' I tell him.

I walk through the gate and close it behind me before realising Tae's still on the other side.

I open the gate and he's standing there, staring. 'Hurry up!' I urge. 'You can't be a scaredy cat if you're going to be a fireman.'

'You know I'm not,' Tae snaps, and runs to join me.

A boy at our school named Ivan called Tae a wuss because he wouldn't jump off the top of the monkey bars, but then Tae did and the whole of Year Three cheered. When it was Ivan's turn, he jumped off and broke his arm and then he screamed and cried and said that he only did it because everyone made him, which wasn't true at all.

I bite my lip. 'I'm sorry,' I tell Tae. 'I didn't mean to call you a scaredy cat. It's just that I really need your help.'

We walk into Frank's little garden. There's no sign of him, which is good. On Saturdays, he likes to sit on his front porch in the sun and read the newspaper, so he shouldn't be roaming the backyard now. The first thing I do is check the aviary in case Mimi has come home on her own. It's still empty.

'What are we doing?' Tae asks.

'You keep watch for Frank and give me a signal if he's coming. I need to borrow some birdseed.'

I hope that my plan will work. I didn't sleep very well last night. My brain was going around and around in circles, worrying about where Mimi could be. Mum says that a worry shared is a worry halved, but I can't make this worry into a fraction yet. I need to do everything I can to get Mimi back on my own first (and by that I mean without any grown-ups).

'Why don't you go and ask Frank for the birdseed?' Tae says. 'I'm sure he'll be happy that we're looking for Mimi. I can wait here.'

I shake my head at Tae and his suggestion. Frank doesn't know that I know Mimi's missing. And he doesn't know it's my fault. My tummy hurts again just thinking about it.

'I have to do this *on my own*,' I growl. Tae looks sad.

Maybe I said that a little too strongly. 'On my own – with you, my amazing assistant.'

Sometimes Tae is a bit sensitive.

Tae smiles. 'Okay. I've got this,' he says, and hides in the bushes by the back door. Then he makes a cooing noise like Mimi does and I jump into the air.

Frank must be coming. I run to Tae and grab his hand. 'Let's go!'

'What's the matter?' he asks, wrinkling his nose.

'You gave me a signal,' I say.

'I was practising,' Tae replies.

'Well, don't.' I frown at him, then run to the little garden shed. There's a big bag of birdseed inside. I haven't got anything to put some in, so we'll have to take the lot. I'll bring the rest back later, once Mimi is found.

I drag the bag out and all the way to the gate, but Tae doesn't meet me. I rest the bag up against the fence and run back to find him. He's playing with a lizard on the path.

'Tae!' I whisper urgently. 'We've got to go.'

He looks up, then gives the lizard one last pat before we scamper to the gate and he finally helps me with the seed. We drag it to my cubbyhouse in the back garden, where no one will notice it's there.

CHAPTER FOUR

Seeds of Hope

'Willa!' Dad calls from the back deck. 'Do you want some morning tea? I've made Anzac biscuits.'

Tae looks at me and nods his head. 'Yes, please. Your dad's the best cook ever.'

That's true (at least when it comes to baking). We bought him a fancy Mixmaster for his birthday and he got very emotional. He said he'd always wanted one, but they were too expensive.

Tae and I have been busy, so we deserve a break. I close the cubby door and we charge across the lawn and up the back steps to where Dad has a plate of biscuits just for us. There's hot Milo too. Woof gets up from his dog bed and wanders over, his tail wagging.

'Hello, Tae, I see you're ready for action,' Dad says.

'We're on a mission,' Tae replies. 'To find –'

'We're doing a special patrol in the neighbourhood.' I cut him off and give him my best googly-eyed stare. 'To make sure that everyone is fire-safe for winter. We don't want any accidents with heaters or electric blankets.'

'That's very grown-up of you,' Dad says with a big smile. 'Are you door-knocking the whole street?'

Tae nods at the exact same time that I shake my head.

I worry about Tae – for someone as clever as he is there are times when he just doesn't get it.

'Looks like you two need to work out your plans,' Dad says.

Inside, the phone rings. Mum answers it, then walks out onto the deck. Dad turns to her at the exact same time that Woof nudges a biscuit from the plate on the table and gobbles it up. I give him a wink. I'm sure he smiles back at me. Woof is not only the best dog in the world, he's also the happiest.

'It's for you, Dan. Emergency. Blocked toilet at Sunset Views. Mrs Scott at number six,' Mum says quietly.

'She had a blocked toilet a couple of

weeks ago after her great-grandson visited and flushed Batman,' Dad says, making sure the mouthpiece is covered. 'Maybe he's been back.'

'Poor Batman,' Mum whispers. Tae and I giggle.

'Smelly Batman,' Tae says, and fans his hand in front of his face.

I laugh out loud. My belly hurts again, but this time in a good way.

'Good morning, Perfect Pipes Plumbing. This is Dan,' Dad says, and walks inside with Mum behind him.

I scoop another biscuit from the table and tell Tae we need to get moving. He follows me, then we hear the side gate creak open. 'Tae, you have to come home, honey. Remember we've got lunch at Nanny and Pa's,' Soo-Min calls as she comes around the side of the house. Mum gives her a wave from the kitchen and walks back outside.

Tae and I have already scampered to the cubby. We can see the two mums through the window. They're talking, which means we might get another few minutes to finish our job. I look at what we've done so far. There seems to be about the same amount of seed on the floor as in the takeaway containers I borrowed from the pantry.

'Sorry I won't be able to help any more,' Tae says.

'That's okay,' I tell him. Maybe Woof can be my assistant (though he'll probably try and eat the seeds, which might be bad for him). I really should finish the plan on my own anyway, seeing that the reason Mimi is missing is because of me.

'Tae!' Soo-Min shouts. 'Hurry up, mate. You know if we're even one minute late, *I'll* be in trouble. Never mind that your father is always the one dragging the chain and Nanny is *his* mother.'

Tae opens the cubby door and waves goodbye.

'Good luck,' he says with a smile. 'I'll bring you some of Nanny's chocolate fudge.'

'Thanks,' I say. The next part of the plan won't be too hard. I just have to carry the containers and put out the seed. Surely that will bring Mimi home.

CHAPTER FIVE

Too Many Birds

I wake up to the sound of the doorbell ringing and parrots screeching.

'Willa,' I hear mum calling. The clock next to the bed says it's half past seven.

I pull the covers over my head. It's Sunday – sleep-in day.

'Willa!'

Mum is standing in the doorway. Suddenly, the rock in my tummy is back.

I pull the covers down a little so just my eyes are showing.

'Hello, Mum,' I mumble. From the look on her face, she's not happy. And I know she hates answering the door in her pyjamas.

'What's the matter?' I ask.

'Come with me,' Mum says, and walks off before I have time to ask anything else.

The bird noises are even louder than before.

I can see Mr Woods from next door standing on the front porch. He's in his dressing gown too. It has a crisscross pattern in red and black.

I walk down the hallway, dragging my feet. Mum is telling him she's terribly sorry and we'll make sure that it never happens again. I have no idea what I've done wrong. Until . . .

Mum turns and looks at me. 'Willa, did you put birdseed everywhere – all up and down the street?'

'I saw her,' Mr Woods says in a mean voice. 'I'm sure it was Willa. I'd recognise those brown plaits and that dog of hers anywhere.'

My eyebrows jump up. It feels like they might fly off the top of my forehead. I don't understand why Mr Woods is cross, unless . . . actually, I really don't know why he's upset at all.

I follow Mum outside. The tiles on the veranda are cold on my bare feet. Mr Woods gives me a super evil glare.

Mum points, and suddenly the reason for all the noise is clear.

There are birds everywhere. Cockatoos, and rosellas, and galahs, and magpies and those little brown ones that dad calls rats with wings. There are budgies too, and I even spot some king parrots. It's as if every bird in the whole of Hibiscus Gardens is in Cricklewood Crescent.

I can't believe it. My plan worked. I scan the street for pigeons. It's hard to see any among all the big birds, but surely Mimi must be there somewhere. I'm sorry that it's noisy, but this is the best news ever.

Mr Woods runs down the front steps onto our lawn with his arms in the air. 'Rah!' he yells.

The birds take off, but they mostly fly to the power lines and onto Tae's roof and the top of Mr Woods' car.

It's then that I notice the lawn isn't just green anymore. It's speckled with hundreds of white blobs. Mr Woods runs over to his driveway and shoos the birds off the car roof.

‘Uh oh,’ I mumble. Mr Woods’ black car is covered in bird poo. It’s everywhere. Some of the poos look like they were done by albatrosses. (They’re the biggest birds in the world. We did a project on them at school.)

Mr Woods spins around. 'And don't get me started on the state of Mrs Woods' washing,' he yells. 'She left it out overnight and now she's going to have to do the whole lot again.'

I bite my lip. My brilliant plan is a disaster.

'I'll fix it,' I whisper.

But I have no idea how.

Mum puts her hand on my shoulder and I burrow into her chest. Even though I'm trying really hard not to, I can't stop the tears. 'I'm sorry,' I sniff. Woof nudges me on the bottom. He always knows when there's a problem.

Mum hugs me tightly and tells Mr Woods that we'll take care of things. I still don't know how.

'Oh, sweetheart, it's okay,' Mum says as the birds start screeching again.

I pull back from her hug and look out at the street. Every car is a mess, and some of the windows and the front porches too. Mr Habib, who lives next door to Tae, is yelling at the birds to pipe down. And Mrs Tan from number two is chasing them with a broom. No one looks very happy.

Mum takes my hand and we head back inside, where at least it's warm and the faces are friendly.

CHAPTER SIX

Help is on Hand

My dad and Sam are up now too.

'Gee, Willa, you've really done a number on the neighbourhood,' my brother says with a chuckle.

'A number two, I'd say.' Dad gives me a wink and a grin.

But I'm not laughing.

'What were you thinking, darling?' Mum asks.

I climb up onto a stool in the

kitchen and tell her and dad and Sam about Mimi, and how she's missing and it's all my fault. I had a really good plan to get her back. At least, I thought it was.

I can't stop my lip from trembling and a tear drops into my mug of hot chocolate.

'Come on, Willa, it's not that bad,' Sam says. He puts his arm around me. 'It won't take too long to give everyone's cars a wash. We can hose down the lawns too, and the verandas and the letterboxes. Mr Habib is always saying he needs to get his windows cleaned.'

I look at my brother in alarm. 'I can't do all that on my own.'

'Dad and I will give you a hand,' Sam says.

Sam is fifteen and he's the best big brother a girl could ever want (most of the time).

'And after that, Willa, you need to go over and tell Frank what happened,' Mum says.

I sigh, and it sounds as if someone has pricked me with a pin. I know she's right. But I still hope I find Mimi out there somewhere among those bazillion birds.

When Tae sees us he comes to help too. He's wearing his fireman's uniform again. He brings his ladder so we can reach up to the high places.

Dad has a really long hose we can drag up and down the street, and he has some special plumber power nozzles. I'm amazed that we're finished by lunchtime. It's lucky our cul-de-sac is short and there are only eight houses.

I didn't scatter any seed at Sunset Views because the manager, Mrs Wilson, was in the garden yesterday afternoon and she was wearing high heels. They always

put her in a bad mood – even worse than usual. Sometimes she growls, and not only at me. At everyone.

The back entrance to Sunset Views is in the circle end of our cul-de-sac. From our place, it looks like there's only a few villas but there's actually more than twenty. There's a nursing home too. The main entrance is on the road around the corner (which is lucky, because sometimes ambulances speed in).

Frank doesn't like the nursing home. That's where his wife was before she died. I never knew her – Soo-Min told me. I know Frank's sad some days, and not just because he has creaky bones and he can't do cartwheels. He misses his wife, and his son and his family who live all the way on the other side of the world in England.

When we're done, Tae goes home because his dad is taking him to buy a new pair of sneakers. Mum makes ham and cheese toasties for lunch and I have a Milo too. I dig the last spoonful from the glass and gulp it down.

'Do you want me to come with you to see Frank?' Mum asks.

I shake my head. 'I'm fine.'

'Make sure that you tell him exactly what happened,' Mum says.

I nod. My tummy hurts again. I looked everywhere for Mimi when we were cleaning up but she wasn't out there. I wonder if Mimi has gone forever – like Norman. I swallow hard, then slide off the stool and drop down onto the floor. Woof stands beside me. Time to tell the truth.

CHAPTER SEVEN

Where's Frank?

I walk through the side gate and into Frank's yard, then check the aviary one last time. Mimi still isn't there.

I make my way up the little path to Frank's back door and knock loudly, but this time when I turn the handle, it's locked. That's strange.

Frank's back door is never locked. It's how I let myself in when I visit. I always knock first, of course, but then I open it and call out. Sometimes Frank doesn't hear the knocking. It's funny. His head is almost bald, but he's got *a lot* of hairs in his ears. Maybe that's the problem. I've offered to trim them, but he hasn't taken me up on that yet.

I press my face against the glass. It's dark inside. All the pigeon stuff is making creepy shadows. Frank's not in his comfy chair in front of the television. He's not

in the kitchen either. He might be having a lie down, but he never does that in the middle of the day. He says nana naps are for *old* people. Frank says a lot of funny things like that.

I walk around to the front of the villa and ring the doorbell. Woof follows right behind, wagging his tail. I can hear the ding-dong chime, but still Frank doesn't come. If I stand up on my tippy toes in the garden bed under the window (being very careful not to trample his favourite flower bush) I can see into his bedroom. He's not there.

I feel even more sick than before. Maybe I had too much Milo, or maybe it's something else.

'Where's Frank?' I ask Woof. He shakes his head. Clearly he doesn't know either.

I have a bad feeling about this. It's not shopping day, and Frank hates bingo, so I know he's not up at the clubhouse with the other residents. One time, when I did convince him to go, he won three packs of toilet rolls and a box of cereal and declared that he was never playing again. As far as I know, he hasn't.

What if he's fallen over in the bathroom and he's hurt? The window is open just a tiny crack. I give it a push and it slides back. I'll pop the screen then climb inside using my gymnastics skills to rescue him. Except that I haven't been practising as much as I should.

'What on earth do you think you're doing, Willa Tait?'

Mrs Wilson's voice scares me so much I jump into the air and the screen falls off into Frank's bedroom. Woof runs away

down the side of the house. He's terrified of Mrs Wilson.

'Um.' I spin around. She's standing right there with her hands on her hips. She does that to the old people too. 'I was looking for Frank.'

Mrs Wilson's eyebrows furrow together like two giant hairy caterpillars and the red curls piled on top of her head flip and flop. She's wearing really high heels too, which isn't a good sign.

'He's probably having a nap,' she says, tapping her foot.

I shake my head. 'He's not,' I tell her.

'And how would you know that?' she asks.

For a moment I'm distracted by a little black hair that's growing out of Mrs Wilson's chin. I wonder if she knows it's there. I think about telling her, then decide maybe now isn't the best time. She glares at me and I remember that she just asked me a question.

'Frank doesn't take nana naps and I've checked all the windows to see if I can find him,' I say.

'Well, you *are* a busybody, Willa Tait,' she snaps. 'Now, off you go home. I've got a good mind to have that gate between your yard and the village blocked up for good.'

She'd better not. It's the quickest way to get to Frank's place. I try and think of something else that will get her attention – maybe *she'll* take a look inside.

'What if Frank's had a fall?' I ask. 'Like Mrs Varma.'

At the mention of the lady's name, Mrs Wilson's shoulders pull back. I twist my lips so they don't make a smile. That was very quick thinking from me.

Mrs Varma was on the floor for almost the whole day before anyone found her, and Mrs Wilson got into trouble with Mrs Varma's family for not taking care of her properly. I heard Soo-Min telling mum.

Mrs Wilson charges up onto Frank's front porch and pulls a keychain from her pocket. Seconds later, she opens the door and calls out.

'Francis, are you here?'

I follow her inside and, while she's checking the bathroom, I dash down the hallway to the lounge room, and the kitchen and the laundry.

Mrs Wilson finds me checking around the side of the washing machine. 'What are you doing in here?' she snaps. Her caterpillar eyebrows are crawling closer together.

'Helping,' I tell her. 'Frank's my friend and I'm worried about him.'

'Frank, I mean Francis,' she corrects herself, 'is a cranky old man. You should have friends your own age.'

'I do,' I reply. 'Tae is my best own-age friend. But Frank is my best old-age friend. And Woof is my best four-legged friend. You can have friends that are all different ages, Mrs Wilson, and different species. There's no law about friends.'

She makes a snorting noise. 'Well, he's clearly not here, is he?'

Mrs Wilson goes back into Frank's bedroom. Maybe she thinks he could be hiding in the wardrobe? I probably would if she came charging into my house.

I open the hall cupboard. 'Frank's suitcase is missing,' I yell. I know he has one because he once had to go to hospital and I saw him get it out.

Mrs Wilson rushes back into the hall and makes a face. 'Well, he certainly didn't let me know he was going anywhere – which is completely against the Sunset Views rules.'

I bite my lip. Just when I thought things couldn't get any worse. Mimi is missing, and now Frank is too.

CHAPTER EIGHT

A New Idea

I trudge up the back steps and into the house. There's a pot bubbling on the stove and Sam's chopping carrots. Mum is reading out a recipe. She says it's important for boys to learn how to cook.

The television is on in the lounge room. I can hear the footy, but I can hear Dad snoring too.

'Did you tell Frank?' Mum asks.

I shake my head. 'He's gone.'

'What?' Sam says, and just misses chopping his thumb.

Mum and Sam look at each other, worry all over their faces.

'Oh dear, I've heard two ambulances going into Sunset Views today,' Mum says.

I frown. 'What are you talking about? Frank's not sick. He's escaped,' I say.

I tell them about Mrs Wilson, and how Frank's suitcase was missing but he didn't check out and Mrs Wilson was even crankier than usual.

I think Frank might have run away to join a troop of acrobats, or maybe he left to become a pirate and sail around the world.

Or maybe he's been kidnapped. I don't like *that* idea one bit.

Mum sighs. 'Oh, thank heavens. For a moment you had me worried, Willa. Then again it is the long weekend. Frank might have decided to take a trip,' Mum says, then goes back to reading the recipe.

I'd forgotten tomorrow was a holiday. That's because it's the Queen's birthday and she gives everyone in Australia a day off, which is really kind because she doesn't even live here.

She probably gives everyone in England the day off too. The other good thing is I have an extra day to find Mimi.

Woof starts barking outside.

'Woof!' Mum yells, but he doesn't stop. 'What's the matter with that silly dog? He's been barking on and off for the past hour.'

There must be something bothering him because, even though his name is Woof, he hardly ever barks at all.

'I'll have a look,' I tell Mum and Sam, and run out onto the back deck. Woof's in the far corner of the yard, near Dad's junk pile. The one that Mum's always telling him to hurry up and get rid of before a snake moves in.

Hopefully Woof hasn't found a snake. They don't usually come out in winter.

'Woof!' I call, but he ignores me and wags his tail like a windscreen wiper.

'Wilfred Connal Tate,' I call again, (that's his 'in trouble' name) but he doesn't pay any attention. He's still barking.

I charge down into the yard and poke around a bit, but I don't like Dad's junk pile. I once had a dream that there was a dragon living under there. That would be much scarier than a snake.

I pull Woof's collar and tell him we can go for a walk. As soon as I say *that* word he stops barking, runs to the deck and goes to grab his lead, which is hanging on a hook.

I clip it to his collar, then wave to Mum.

'We're going to the dog park,' I yell.

'Take Tae. He came looking for you when you were over at Frank's – I forgot to mention it,' Mum calls, and blows me a kiss.

I walk down the driveway and see Soo-Min. She's coming out their front door dressed in her work uniform. I give a wave and ask if Tae can come with me and Woof. Soo-Min smiles. She ducks back inside for a second then tells me Tae's on his way.

A minute later he runs out and meets me on the footpath. He's still a fireman, but now he has really cool red and blue striped runners. I don't think firemen wear those but I don't tell him that.

'Is Mimi back?' he asks.

I shake my head. 'Frank's gone too,' I tell him, then explain what happened.

'We should make some posters and put them in everyone's letterboxes,' Tae says. 'We can do it on the computer and Dad can print them out.'

I nod at Tae. That's an excellent plan. Maybe someone has caught Mimi and put her in a cage. She's really friendly so that could have happened. 'I can draw a picture.' For the first time in a while, my tummy doesn't feel quite as squirmy – which is a good thing.

'Do you want to do it now? Dad's not busy,' Tae says.

Woof is dancing about on his lead.

'Let's go to the park first and we can do it when we come back,' I say in my normal voice. Then I whisper to Tae. 'Woof gets upset if I tell him we're going for a walk and then we don't.'

Tae gives Woof a pat.

'He just smiled at me, Willa,' Tae says.

'Of course he did. He's Woof,' I reply as we set off for the park.

CHAPTER NINE

Have You Seen This Pigeon?

There was a moment at the dog park where I thought we'd found Mimi. But then I realised the pigeon I was staring at had a black stripe on its belly and Mimi's tummy is plain grey.

Now we're back at Tae's house. Woof is having a sleep under the table where Tae and I are working. Tae just blamed him for doing a stinky pop off, but I think it was Tae. He eats a lot of beans.

'What do you think?' I show Tae my picture.

'That eye is a bit wonky,' he says. 'And she's too skinny.'

'Argh, that's the fifth one.' I sigh loudly. 'This is taking too long. We won't have time to deliver the posters if I can't even finish the drawing.'

I scrunch up the page and throw it on the table with the other rejects, then get a fresh piece of paper and start again.

I think really hard about what Mimi looks like.

Tae is drawing too, but his picture is a fire station, which isn't any use for the poster.

'Hey, kids, I need some help,' Tae's dad, Mark, calls out from his study down the hall.

Tae slips off his chair. I'm right behind him.

Mark's a drama teacher at Sam's high school. Mum says that he used to be on a TV show called *Surfside High* when she was a teenager. All the girls at her school had a big crush on him. That's so weird to me, because he's just Tae's dad.

'Does this look like Mimi?' Mark asks, pointing at the computer screen.

I peer at the picture. 'I think that *is* Mimi.'

'I hate to break it to you, Willa, but lots of pigeons look alike,' Mark says.

'It's better than this.'

I show him my latest drawing and he smiles and tells me it's really good, but I know he's being kind. Grown-ups say stuff like that all the time, but us kids are not as silly as they think we are.

'Why don't we use this photo, and you can tell me the words to go on the poster?' Mark says.

That's a great idea. I should have thought of that before. Maybe it's smarter *not* to try and do everything on my own.

'Okay,' I nod and bite my lip. 'Mmm.'

I try to remember what sort of things we put on our posters last week about a character from the book we were reading at school.

'What about this?' I say. Mark writes down what I tell him.

'We need to put a phone number too, but it's probably best not to put my name or address,' I say.

'That's good thinking, Willa,' Mark says. 'Just a phone number is very sensible.'

'We should offer a reward,' Tae says.

I frown. I only have five dollars in my piggy bank, and I was saving that up to buy Mum's birthday present.

I shake my head. 'I don't have enough money.'

'I'll chip in twenty dollars,' Mark says.

'But that's so much,' I say, biting my lip and feeling bad because it's my fault Mimi is missing. It's not fair for Mark to spend his money on my problems. 'I promise I'll pay you back.'

MISSING

MIMI THE PIGEON

COLOUR: GREY WITH PURPLE AND GREEN ON HER NECK

SOUNDS: COO COO

LOVES: A SCRATCH UNDER HER CHIN AND EATING BIRD SEED

HATES: CATS (ESPECIALLY GINGER BISCUIT WHEN SHE SITS OUTSIDE HER CAGE AND LICKS HER LIPS)

'It's okay, Willa,' Mark says with a grin. 'Tae won't get to go on the excursion to the zoo next week, but he won't mind.'

Tae's mouth flaps open. 'What! I've already got my zookeeper outfit ready,' Tae shouts. Then his dad gives him a wink and we both realise that Mark's just kidding. We should have known, because he makes jokes and plays tricks a lot.

Mark finishes the poster and prints enough so that we can put them in all the letterboxes around the neighbourhood.

We carry the pages in a little shopping bag that Tae puts over his shoulder. Woof comes too. He's going to be really tired tonight after doing this *and* going to the dog park, especially because his best friend Link was there. He's a sausage dog, and he loves chasing Woof and running in and out of his legs. Woof always just smiles. That's because he's the gentlest dog in the world as well as the happiest.

I fold the page and put the first flyer into Mr and Mrs Habib's letterbox. Then I remember today is Sunday and tomorrow is a holiday, so no one will check their boxes until Tuesday. We'll have to knock on the doors and deliver them properly. It's the only way.

The trouble is, because its Sunday, lots of people are out. We put the flyers under the front door if no one answers. A couple of people tell us they think they've seen Mimi, but they're not really sure. Tae also asks everyone if they're fire-safe for winter. Mrs Tan says she needs new batteries in her smoke alarms, and Tae offers to bring his dad over tomorrow to fix them.

I hope the flyers work, or I don't know if we'll ever see Mimi again.

CHAPTER TEN

Good News

Tae's staying at my house for a sleepover. Our mums organised it yesterday as a surprise. Tae and I have lots of sleepovers. Sometimes Sam and Dad help us put up the tent in the back yard, but Mum says it's too cold tonight.

Sam's baked dinner smells delicious and there's butterscotch pudding and custard for dessert. My favourites.

We just sit down to eat when the telephone rings.

Dad hops up to get it. (It's always for him at dinnertime – mostly emergencies with broken taps, or blocked toilets or burst pipes, like the man in the next street over whose whole yard turned into a swimming pool one night.)

Mum sighs.

Dad answers the phone and frowns. He says 'yes' and 'mmm' and then smiles.

'That's wonderful. We'll be around in an hour to collect her.'

Dad hangs up the phone and turns back to the table. 'It looks like Mimi is coming home.'

Tae and I turn to each other and cheer loudly.

'The posters worked,' Tae says, high-fiving me.

'I knew they would,' I tell him. 'That picture your dad found was perfect.'

'Frank will be happy,' Mum says as I hop down from my chair. 'Where are you going, darling?'

'To get Mimi,' I say.

Dad shakes his head. 'Not before we eat. Your brother's been cooking all afternoon.'

'Yeah, it took me hours to get that pudding perfect,' Sam replies with a grin.

It does smell really good, but my leg is jiggling up and down as I wait. I really want to get Mimi.

Of course, everyone eats as slow as snails tonight. Tae's still got half of his pudding left when I gobble the last bite of mine and stand up.

'I'm sure that Woof would enjoy some of that,' I say, glancing at Tae's plate.

'No way.' Tae frowns. 'This is *so* good.'

I give him my best googly-eyed stare. Tae doesn't get it. He might be the smartest kid in our class, but sometimes he has no idea.

Woof is barking again. I run to the door and call out for him to stop. Something is really bothering him down at Dad's junk pile. He keeps on barking until I put the leftovers in his bowl and he runs back to the deck to gobble it up.

WOOF
WOOF
WOOF!
woof

Finally Dad stands up. He walks to the kitchen and starts filling the kettle.

'Can't you have a cup of tea when we get back?' I ask. I don't think I can wait any longer. We need to get Mimi now, so I know she's really safe.

Dad grins at me. 'Oh, okay. You do know that Mimi won't have any idea if we're a couple of minutes late?'

'Yes she will. She's a very clever pigeon,' I say, and run back to drag Tae from his chair. We're in the car before Dad has left the house. Then I remember we need something to put Mimi in. I find an old washing basket and a towel in the garage. We can put the towel over the top of the basket, and the slats on the side mean there's plenty of breathing holes.

Dad finally hops into the car and we

set off. It's not far at all – we pull into a driveway just around the corner.

I know who lives here. It's a boy from our school called Robbie. He's in Year Five. Mum says he spends more time with our principal, Mr Newton, than anyone else at school.

She knows that because she's the office lady, and the office lady knows everything. Mum says that her job is a bit like being a nurse, an organiser, a counsellor and a spy all at the same time. You have to be good at putting on bandaids, helping everything run smoothly, making people feel better and keeping everyone's secrets.

Suddenly I remember that we offered a reward and I don't have any money. I tell Dad. It's lucky he has his wallet.

The three of us hop out of the car. I take the washing basket and the towel

with me and follow Dad to the front door. Tae is behind me.

Dad rings the bell and we wait. There's a dog barking inside and someone is shouting. It sounds like an argument. Poor Mimi. I hope she's not too upset by all that yelling.

A man opens the door. He has greasy hair and is wearing tracksuit pants with holes in the knees. There are stains on his jumper – maybe he spilt his dinner down the front. He peers out the door, staring past us as if he's expecting someone else.

'What do you want?' he asks in a gruff voice.

I really don't like his tone, and I can tell Dad doesn't either.

'We've come to get Mimi,' I say.

'Who's Mimi?'

'Frank's pigeon,' I tell him, but that doesn't seem to ring any bells.

'A boy called and said that he'd found a missing pigeon,' Dad says.

'Oh, I think you want the young bloke. Robbie!' he shouts. But Robbie doesn't come. 'Wait here,' the man says, and slams the door.

CHAPTER ELEVEN

But That's Not . . .

We wait for a really long time. There's more shouting and the sound of running feet and then another door slams. Robbie's big brother, Jacko, scurries out through the side gate and turns down the street, pulling a hoodie over his head. He's best friends with Michael Woods, who lives next door to us. They always look as if they're up to something.

'Hey, mate,' Dad calls out. 'Is your brother coming?'

But Jacko just raises his hand and gives a backwards wave. He doesn't even turn around. He's got no manners at all – like the man who slammed the door in our faces.

I turn and see that Tae has gone back to the car. I can't blame him – it's cold. Dad is about to knock again when finally the door opens and Robbie is standing there. There's a bucket with a tea towel over the top next to him. I hope that's not where Mimi is.

'Have you got my reward?' he asks.

Dad has the twenty dollars in his hand. Robbie holds his palm out, but I shake my head.

'Could we please see Mimi?' I ask.

'She's asleep,' Robbie says. 'If you wake her up, she'll go crazy like when I was trying to catch her.'

'I'll be quiet,' I say, reaching for the bucket.

'Reward first,' Robbie says.

Dad steps in. 'I think we need to see Mimi, then you can have your money,' he says firmly.

Robbie reluctantly hands over the bucket. I peer inside.

'No way!' I gasp. 'This bird is stuffed.'

'Willa! Language! You don't say things like that,' Dad says, then he looks at it too.

'Oh, yes I see what you mean.' He frowns.

Inside the bucket is a stuffed pigeon.

'It's exactly the same as the one in the picture!' Robbie protests. 'You didn't say it had to be alive.'

I sigh. 'On the poster, it said the noises that Mimi makes and that she likes a scratch under the chin. I don't think that pigeon has made a noise for a very long time.'

I can't believe it. Just when we thought Mimi was found. Now I feel even worse, as if someone has punched me in the stomach really hard. I've failed. We're never going to find Mimi and Frank is going to be sadder than ever.

Dad puts his hand on my shoulder and we turn to leave.

'What about my twenty bucks?' Robbie says.

Dad and I look back at him.

'You didn't find Mimi,' I say.

Robbie's shoulders slump and he pulls a mean face.

A woman yells from inside. 'Robbie, where's Roma the Pigeon? You haven't taken her out of the china cabinet again, have you?'

Robbie slams the door and I shake my head.

'Don't worry, Willa. We'll find Mimi,' Dad says as we walk to the car, but I'm not so sure. Tae's fallen asleep – lucky for him. I can't imagine I'm going to get any rest until Mimi is safely home.

CHAPTER TWELVE

Mimi

Even though my eyes are closed, my brain won't stop thinking. It hasn't stopped all night. Where's Mimi? Where's Frank? Are they ever coming back? Maybe Frank really did run away to be a pirate? His limp is real, and he does already have a patch from when he had to have an operation on his eye.

The galahs have started screeching and it's getting light outside. There's no chance I'll be able to sleep now. Tae and I weren't allowed to put the tent up in the yard, so Sam helped us set up a camp in the family room at the back of the house instead. My bed is on the lounge and Tae is in Sam's swag on the floor. I decide that a smile from Woof might cheer me up. I kneel on the lounge and look outside.

But Woof isn't in his bed, which is odd because he usually never gets up before me. I peer down into the yard. He's laying down at the junk pile. He's not barking and waking up the whole neighbourhood, but it does sound like he's crying.

I'm just about to head outside when Tae pipes up. He makes me jump. I didn't realise he was awake.

'Where are you going, Willa?' he asks.

'There's something upsetting Woof,' I whisper.

'I'll come with you,' Tae says.

We tiptoe out the door and down the stairs to the yard. I'm surprised Woof doesn't get up to come and meet us.

I peer at him, wondering why he's acting so weird. 'Tae! Look!' I gasp.

Under Woof's chest are some shiny grey feathers.

'Uh oh,' Tae says.

I lean down closer. It's a bird. A pigeon. Woof moves back a bit. I'm pretty sure it's Mimi.

'Is it alive?' Tae asks. I can't blame him for asking after our earlier disappointment with Robbie (but Woof doesn't eat birds for snacks, no matter what Tae might think).

Mimi blinks at me and Woof nuzzles against her. She doesn't seem to mind, which is strange. Most birds run away from him. That's because he's really big, and sometimes a bit too friendly. I wonder if this is why he was barking down at the junk pile yesterday. If only I'd taken a closer look. Maybe Mimi was here all along.

'Good boy, Woof,' I tell him.

I reach in and touch Mimi's head. My tummy doesn't feel sick anymore, and my heart feels like it's going to burst with happiness.

'What should we do?' Tae asks.

'Take her home,' I say. 'Hopefully Frank will come back soon. She'll be there when he arrives.'

'Do you want the laundry basket?' Tae says.

I shake my head. 'I'll carry her. I hold her all the time.'

I reach in and gently scoop the pigeon up. Woof doesn't take his eyes off her.

We walk to the gate that goes to Frank's place. Tae pushes it open. He has to open the aviary too.

'There you go, Mimi.' I set her down carefully on one of the little perches inside and make sure that she has seed and water.

'That's a relief,' Tae says. 'Frank will be so happy when he comes back.'

I nod, only half paying attention as I'm looking at Mimi and wondering what's different about her. Then I realise.

She just stood up.

'Oh, Mimi,' I gasp. 'What happened to you?'

Tae studies her more closely too. 'Where's her leg?'

Suddenly I feel hot and a bit sick again.

'You don't think Woof ate it, do you?' Tae says.

I frown. Woof loves his food but I can't imagine even he'd be keen on a skinny little pigeon leg.

'No, he was looking after her,' I say. 'Maybe it was a shark? Or more likely it was Ginger Biscuit. I saw that serial killer in the garden yesterday, stalking a bush turkey.'

'Wow – Mimi's lucky to be alive,' Tae says. 'Imagine a shark biting off a pigeon's leg.'

'That would be scary,' I say.

'Hey, Willa.' Tae prods my arm. 'Look!'

I turn to see what he's talking about and freeze. There's a light on in Frank's villa, and the back door has just opened.

I really don't want Frank to find us in the aviary, but he's heading this way.

'Who's there?' he growls. 'What are you doing? Show yourself!'

I look at Tae and he looks at me. 'Uh oh,' we both say at exactly the same time.

CHAPTER THIRTEEN

Medals and Muddles

'Quick!' I whisper to Tae, and we close the aviary door. 'I don't want Frank to see Mimi yet – not until he's prepared. It will be a big shock.'

'Frank! You're back!' I shout, and run towards him, hugging him tightly around the middle. 'Did the kidnappers let you go because you were too grumpy? Or did you forget the eyepatch that you needed to be a pirate?'

Frank looks at me and frowns. His eye bags are bigger than ever.

'What are you talking about, Willa? I wasn't kidnapped. I made a last minute trip to the city for a special dinner,' Frank says.

That makes sense. Going to the city always makes me tired too.

'That's a relief. I knew that you wouldn't really have joined an acrobat troop, seeing that you can't do cartwheels at all,' I say. 'But Mrs Wilson is very upset. You didn't sign out.'

'Pff,' Frank rolls his eyes. 'Last time I heard, Sunset Views was a retirement village, not a prison.'

The kettle is whistling inside. Frank turns to go.

'Come on then,' he says. 'This is early, even by your standards, Willa, but I might as well make us all some tea.'

Tae hangs back.

I give him a nudge. 'It's okay,' I whisper.

Sometimes I visit Frank early in the morning because he gets up before the sun and there are days I do too. Breakfast at Frank's is vegemite toast and sweet milky tea. Mum won't make it because she says four scoops of sugar is three too many.

'When did you get home?' I ask as Frank busies himself in the kitchen.

'Very late last night. My friend asked me to stay longer, but the traffic was giving me the heebie jeebies and I had to get back for Mimi,' Frank says.

I have to tell him what happened. It's all my fault that Mimi has a pirate leg now. My mouth is dry and my palms are sweaty, but there's no point waiting any longer. I take a deep breath and am just about to confess when Tae pipes up.

'What's this?' he asks, then picks up a frame on the kitchen table and shows it to me. Inside is a gold medal with a pigeon on it and a plaque with some fancy writing. It says, 'Awarded to Francis Pickles for lifetime service to the Pigeon Racing Society of Australia.'

'Frank, you got a gold medal!' I say excitedly. 'Except they called you Francis and you hate that name.'

'It's nothing,' Frank says, and bats his hand in the air.

'Yes it is. A gold medal says you're the best,' I say.

'Doesn't mean much now that Mimi's the only bird I have left,' Frank replies, setting the tea cups down in front of me and Tae.

I'm really glad that Mimi's back, but I still can't bring myself to tell Frank that she's a bit lighter than when she left. If only Tae hadn't noticed Frank's medal, I'd have said something by now. It's just so hard – poor Frank's already lost Norman and now poor Mimi's lost a leg.

Frank brings the toast out, and for a few minutes we sit and drink our tea and eat our toast in silence. Frank must think it's strange, seeing as I usually talk all the time.

He glances at the pigeon clock on the wall.

'Mimi should be back soon,' he says.

'She's already here,' Tae blurts, and I kick him under the table.

'Ow!' he yells.

Frank looks at me. 'I wish you'd said something earlier. Every second counts,' he says, and hops up from the table.

I don't know what he's talking about. Frank heads outside and I follow, with Tae behind. I want to get to the aviary first and tell Frank what happened before he gets a huge shock. It might give him a heart attack or something, and then that would be all my fault too.

But just as Frank is about to reach the aviary, there's a flapping sound and a pigeon swoops down from high in the sky to the ledge on the outside of the coop.

'There you are, my girl,' Frank says. He reaches into his pocket and pulls out a little machine, then waves it near the tag on the pigeon's leg.

'Is *that* Mimi?' I gasp.

'First race in a year. She's done well,' Frank says, checking his watch.

'Race? What race?' I ask, my eyebrows jumping up.

Tae stares at the pigeon on the ledge and then back at me.

I know he's thinking the same thing I am. *What's going on?*

'I decided to enter Mimi in a race on the weekend. Seeing as I was getting the award and all,' Frank says. 'I sent her off on Friday.'

'So it's not my fault that she was missing?' I ask. I can't believe it.

Frank frowns at me. 'She was never missing, Willa, you silly chook. Why on earth would you think that?'

I look at the aviary and at Tae.

'Well, who's that we found?' Tae asks.

Frank peers inside to see.

CHAPTER FOURTEEN

A Celebration

'Hurry up, Frank!' I call as I run along the path to his back door. 'Dinner's almost ready.'

I knock, then walk inside. Frank is standing at the kitchen table, holding the frame with his medal.

'Come on. Everyone else is already there,' I say. Frank hasn't even put his cardigan on yet and he always fiddles with the buttons for ages.

'I don't know, Willa,' he says. 'I'm a bit tired.'

That's obvious – those eye bags of his haven't got any smaller since this morning.

'But Dad's baked a cheesecake and the barbecue is already on,' I say. 'It's a celebration. For your gold medal, and Mimi's race and, you know.'

'I don't like a fuss,' Frank says, smoothing his hair.

'Me either, but when people go to a lot of trouble it's bad manners not to go,' I say.

That's not completely true. Well, it's true about the bad manners, but I love it when Mum and Dad and Sam make a big fuss of my birthday or if I do something good at school. I just don't want to sound like a princess. (Which, clearly, I'm not.)

Frank straightens his tie and puts his cardigan on. Thank goodness he doesn't do up the buttons. Then he turns around.

'You look very nice,' I say, and run over to grab his hand. We walk outside together. Woof is there, waiting for us. Frank closes the door, but he doesn't bother to lock it. He always says it's lucky we live in a good neighbourhood. Mostly I'd agree, except for Michael Woods and Robbie and his big brother.

We walk past the aviary and I stop.

'Frank!' I point at Mimi.

Sitting nuzzled beside her is Norman. I could hardly believe it when Frank said the pigeon Woof found was him. But it said so on his tag (lucky it was on his good leg). He's been gone for four years. Norman and Mimi could be twins, except for the missing leg, but Frank told me they were husband and wife. Pigeons fall in love for the whole of their lives. When Norman went missing, Mimi was heartbroken. I think Frank was too.

Frank gives my hand a squeeze. 'Thanks for finding him, Willa – and you too, Woof.' He gives Woof a pat on the top of his shaggy head. It means a lot.' Frank brushes his eye. I think there might have been a tear in it. There's one in mine too.

'I love you, Frank Pickles,' I say.

Frank grunts. I don't care that he doesn't say it back because I know he loves me too.

'We should tell the newspaper about Norman and Mimi and your medal,' I say.

'Oh no you don't, young lady. There will be no stories in the paper,' Frank says.

'But why not? It's a miracle. It might even be on the front page,' I say as we walk through the gate into our back yard. Woof wags his tail and pushes ahead, running up onto the deck, where Dad's taking care of the barbecue. 'I can see it now. "Norman the pigeon escapes a shark attack and finds his way home to his wife Mimi after four years, and Frank wins a gold medal and Mimi wins a race." That might be a bit long for the headline but I'm sure they could fix it.'

Frank laughs. I feel like I just won the lottery.

'G'day, Frank,' Dad calls out.

'Congratulations on your award,' says Mark, and shakes his hand.

Frank nods. I couldn't say for sure, but I think there might even be a bit of a grin on his lips.

Woof runs back down the steps with a stolen sausage in his mouth. Dad hasn't noticed, but I see him. He hides behind me. I turn and give him a scowl, but then I wink and he gobbles it up. 'I'll get you another one later,' I tell him. Woof smiles at me. He really is the best four-legged friend in the whole wide world.

'Hi, Tae.' I wave, though I'm a bit confused – he's not a fireman anymore. Then I remember today is Monday, and Tae always dresses up as a new person of

greatness at the start of the week. But this one is different to his usual fireman and cowboys.

He's wearing a pair of cream-coloured trousers and a shirt and tie with a cardigan over the top. Tae looks like an old man.

'Who are you this week?' I ask.

'I'm Frank,' Tae says. 'Because he's a person of greatness too.'

I smile at Frank as Mum passes him a drink.

'That's a very good choice,' I say. 'Maybe your best one ever.'

About the Author

Jacqueline Harvey has had a passion for storytelling since she was a child and writes books filled with adventure, mystery, humour and heart. A former teacher, she is the author of the popular Alice-Miranda, Clementine Rose and Kensy and Max series. Joining these beloved characters are Jacqueline's newest works – *That Cat* and the Willa and Woof series.

jacquelineharvey.com.au